An Amish Wedding

To Henry and Annie, Cari and Tom, and newlyweds everywhere.
—R. A.

This book is dedicated to my mother and father with love.
—P. P.

The author wishes to thank Sara, Lydia, Fannie, Amy Sprout, and Marcia.
The illustrator thanks Lauren Vaughn and Anita Sander for modeling as the little sister and bride,
and everyone else who helped out.

Atheneum Books for Young Readers
An imprint of Simon & Schuster Children's Publishing Division
1230 Avenue of the Americas
New York, New York 10020

Text copyright © 1998 by Richard Ammon
Illustrations copyright © 1998 by Pamela Patrick

Book design by Nina Barnett

The text of this book is set in Weiss

First Edition

Printed in the United States of America

10   9   8   7   6   5   4   3   2   1

Library of Congress Cataloging in Publication Data
Ammon, Richard.
An Amish wedding / Richard Ammon; illustrated by Pamela Patrick.
p.   cm.
ISBN 0-689-81677-4
1. Amish—Marriage customs and rites—Juvenile literature.
I. Patrick, Pamela. II. Title.
E184.M45A45   1998
392.5'088'287—dc21
97-9740
CIP   AC

AN AMISH WEDDING

by RICHARD AMMON
illustrated by PAMELA PATRICK

ATHENEUM BOOKS FOR YOUNG READERS

My sister Anna is getting married!

In late spring when the strawberry patch was full of blossoms, Samuel asked her to be his wife.

But they won't tell a soul until they are published on the second Sunday after fall communion. That's when the congregation listens with quiet excitement while the minister announces the names of couples who plan to be married.

I knew when Mamm asked me to help plant all that extra celery, enough to serve at a wedding dinner.

Anna will be married right here, in our home. This summer, Datt finally got around to putting down a concrete floor in the basement and fixing that rickety banister. When we weren't making hay, my brother Jake and I painted the house. I liked smearing on the bright white paint. Datt said I painted more of myself than the house.

In the cool summer evenings Anna sewed her wedding dress.

Choosing the day for the wedding was not easy. Amish weddings are held in November, after harvest but before winter weather sets in. They're held only on Tuesdays or Thursdays, so the bride's family has a day to get ready and a day to *redd-up*.

After deciding on the first Tuesday in November, Anna sat at the kitchen table and wrote invitations to aunts and uncles who don't go to our church. She even invited a few English friends.

I helped Anna address the envelopes and lick the stamps. Whew! I didn't know she knew so many people outside the valley.

A few Sundays ago Samuel and Anna drove through the valley brimming with crisp autumn colors. At Ben Lapp's place they gathered with their gang for the last time as singles to sing slow hymns and other songs in German.

Singings are a time for eating pretzels and popcorn, sipping cider, and getting acquainted. One Sunday two years ago, Samuel asked Anna if he could drive her home afterwards. That evening she climbed into his open buggy, and they've been seeing each other ever since.

By breakfast time, I knew this was no ordinary Monday morning. All my aunts and uncles streamed into the kitchen at the same moment. My aunts scurried down to the basement to make ready for the wedding dinner. Uncle Steve and Uncle Amos began carrying out most of our furniture and storing it in the cleaned-up workshop. When Uncle David pulled up with the wagon stacked with the benches for church, Uncle Jake opened the doors between the sitting room and the large kitchen. Steve and Amos helped David unload the benches, which Jake arranged in neat rows.

As my brother Danny and I started for school, we saw Samuel walking toward the chicken coop, carrying an axe. I decided not to look back.

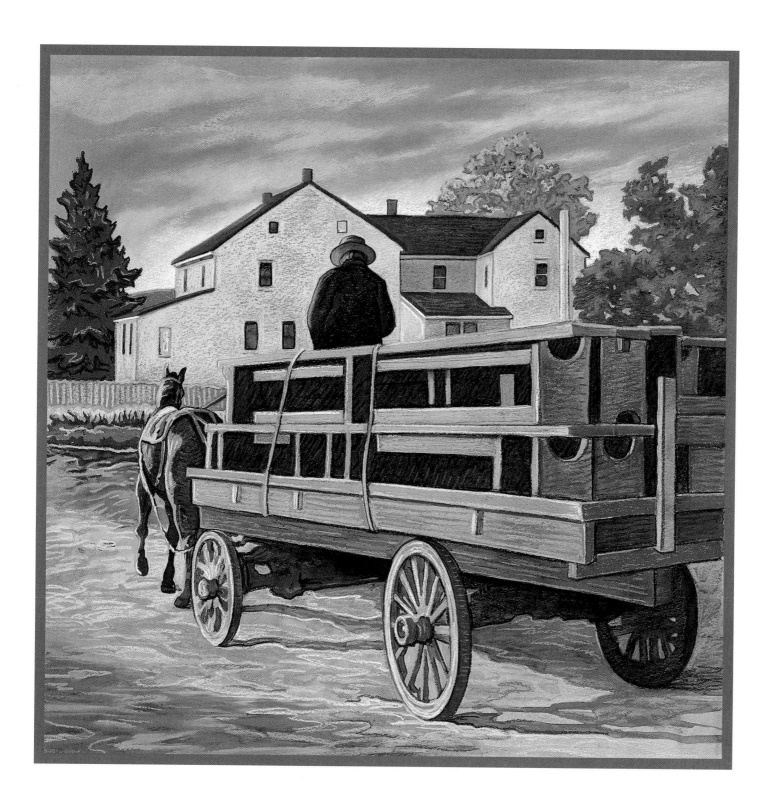

This morning I bounce out of bed. The weather's dreary, but no one will mind. This is Anna's wedding day!

Some of our aunts and uncles are here already. Some will serve as ushers, or *Forgehers*. In the basement Aunt Lydia begins cooking thirty-five chickens for dinner, while Aunt Lizzie dices the celery.

Talking as fast as they work, Aunt Fannie and Aunt Rachel wiggle their knives, spiraling out long curls of potato skins. It's good they work fast because they must peel enough potatoes to feed three hundred people. Ha, I'd rather milk forty cows than peel that many potatoes!

I dash upstairs and peek out the window. "They're coming!" I call out as I see the first in a long line of gray buggies drawn by chestnut horses high-stepping down our lane.

Danny and five cousins greet each driver. The boys look so grown-up, unhitching the horses and leading them into the barn.

Within the long line of gray buggies are several vans carrying friends and relatives from faraway districts. Our English neighbors are driving the only car.

Samuel and Anna and their *Newesitzers*, the bridal party, greet the guests as they arrive. Our aunts and uncles lead the guests to their seats, the men to one side and the women to the other. After awhile Samuel and Anna go upstairs to meet with the ministers.

As we sing "Lob Lied," a traditional hymn, Samuel and Anna come down the stairs.

At the end of the sermon, Samuel and Anna stand and step forward, holding hands. Bishop Levi places his hands above and below theirs and leads them in saying their vows. No rings are exchanged because we Amish do not wear jewelry of any kind.

Levi then says, "Go forth in the name of the Lord. You are now man and wife."

Taking their seats, Samuel and Anna seem to glow like sunshine on this cloudy day.

The moment we finish singing the closing hymn, the room shudders and thunders as our uncles move benches, fitting three into a brace to make a table. Just as quickly, our aunts fling white cloths over the tables and set out plates and silverware.

Within a few minutes, the room is turned into a huge dining room. But it's still not big enough for everyone to eat at once. The bride and groom and their families eat first. I sit with Datt and Mamm. Today they do not have to lift a finger.

Samuel and Anna and their *Newesitzers* sit in a special corner called the *Eck*.

I realize how hungry I am when our aunts and uncles bring out platters of steaming roast chicken and cooked celery.

"*Des fersuchts so gut* (This tastes so good)," I exclaim.
Aunt Lydia carries the wedding cake to the *Eck.*
Spelled out in pink and blue icing are the words "Best
Wishes Anna and Samuel." After Aunt Lydia serves
everyone in the *Eck,* only a few slices are left. I don't
worry because our aunts have baked plenty of other
cakes, *more* than enough for everyone.

After dinner the men drift to the shop next to the barn, where they talk about crops and livestock.

Anna goes upstairs to take off her black cap and put on a white cap. She will never again wear her black cap. After today her white apron and cape will be put away until her funeral.

While she is changing, my cousin Rachel and I hurry to my bedroom to get the broom I hid there last evening. We tiptoe down the hall to Anna's door and lay the broom handle across the doorway. We wait patiently, trying hard not to giggle.

We can hear Fannie ask Anna if she wants to go look at the wedding presents that her English and single friends brought. As Anna steps over the broom handle, we squeal with delight. She has just passed from maiden to homemaker.

When most of the guests have returned, Uncle Jake sings the first few notes of a familiar hymn and everybody joins in. These hymns are sung so slowly that it takes almost fifteen minutes to sing all the verses. But Samuel and Anna do not sing. Sitting in the *Eck*, they open gifts of candy sculptures in pretty little dishes. Each dish of candy represents a special gift for Samuel and Anna. Someone has taken time to make them a present of a hard candy horse pulling a pretzel wagon with marshmallow wheels.

While the grownups sing, Rachel, Danny, Cousin Omar, and I go outside and sneak up to the window next to Anna. When we tap on the pane, Anna cracks open the window and slips us some of the candy. We dash off to divide up our treats. But soon we're back for more.

In the evening, the order for serving dinner is reversed. The guests from far away are seated first, then the relatives.

While the others are eating, those soon to be married and the teens gather upstairs. With great care and thought, Anna matches couples.

Downstairs the tables are cleared. Clean dishes and silverware are set out.

When everything is ready, everybody gathers to watch this special moment. First, Samuel and Anna come down the stairs, smiling as if they can't hide a secret. Right behind them are the *Newesitzers* and those couples who will be married later this month.

I stand on my tiptoes and crane my neck to see the parade of unmarried couples. Sometimes it's a surprise to see who is paired with whom.

After the couples sit down, our uncles and aunts serve a casserole of meat and crackers, along with platters of vegetables—mashed potatoes, corn, peas, and cabbage slaw.

Those in the *Eck* receive a special treat—ice cream! Each couple shares a dish. Samuel and Anna pretend to argue about who gets the last spoonful. Anna wins out, but I don't think Samuel minds.

As our aunts clear the last plates, leaving only platters of cakes and cookies, Uncle Steve refills Datt's coffee cup.

Uncle Amos and Uncle David hand out copies of hymnals with the faster songs not sung during church services. Uncle Jake intones the first words, *"Nun sich der Tag,"* and the room fills with the melody of "Amazing Grace."

Most of our guests have gone home, but a few still linger to bend Datt's ear. Around ten-thirty I climb the stairs, almost too tired to undress.

Samuel and Anna stayed with us last night.

In the morning they're awake at four o'clock to help *redd-up*. But before Anna can wash the tablecloths and towels, she and Samuel must unravel the wash line that pranksters have twisted and draped through the maple tree.

I wish I could stay to see all the other tricks their friends have planned for them, but I must go to school. *"Kum,* Daniel," I call. *"Es ist Tzeit in die Schul geh* (It's time to go to school)."

Amish newlyweds do not go on a honeymoon, but every weekend during the winter they visit their relatives. On these visits Samuel and Anna will be given their wedding presents. Uncle Steve has made Samuel a desk, and Uncle David has made them a bed.

In the spring when they set up housekeeping, Samuel will begin growing a beard.

Now that the house is almost back in order, I sit in the rocker by the stove remembering yesterday, looking forward to more weddings, and thinking of a day that seems so far off—my own wedding day.

Author's Note

The author has been fortunate enough to be invited to several Old Order Amish weddings. The customs represented in this book are those practiced by Lancaster County (Pennsylvania) Old Order Amish. While this community is not in Lancaster County, all the parents and grandparents were born and raised in Lancaster County. Customs and traditions in other Old Order Amish communities will vary. For example, buggy shapes and colors, men's suspenders, and women's caps and capes differ according to community: Big Valley (Pennsylvania), Nebraska (Pennsylvania), Delaware, Ohio, Indiana, Ontario, and so on. These differences are addressed in two books by Stephen Scott: *Why Do They Dress That Way* (Good Books, 1986) and *Plain Buggies* (Good Books, 1981).